Where's Larry This Time?

Philip Barrett

Colourist: Ken Mahon

THE O'BRIEN PRESS
DUBLIN

Can you find my family & friends?

Larry the Leprechaun and his family are taking a trip around Ireland – leprechauns go on holidays too, don't you know? – and they're going to some very scenic and exciting places.

Being a real Irish leprechaun, Larry has relatives all over the country and he'll be looking out for them – or trying to avoid them – wherever he goes. (If you'd like to look out for these rapscallions, check them out towards the back of the book.) See if you can spot Larry and his wife and children; leprechauns are small fellows, so they're hard to spot, but look out for their distinctive green outfits.

If you spot his crock of gold, though, don't even think about stealing it! A leprechaun's life's work is hiding and protecting their gold where humans can't find it, but if you look hard you might see it glinting away.

Larry the Leprechaun
The one and only.

Laura the Leprechaun
Larry's wife can teach even him a few things about hiding.

Lar Junior
Larry's son prefers a more modern leprechaun outfit.

Larrissa
If she wanted you to find her you'd know about it.

Larry's Crock of Gold
Each crock also has four gold coins hidden around it.

Larry's Magic Watch
The past and present get a little mixed up!

The Tour Bus
It may be old, but it gets into some surprising places.

Jenny the Bus Driver
She loves her cup of tea after a long drive.

The Busker
Sometimes people love his songs, sometimes they don't.

The Golfer
He's mad about golf - but that doesn't make him good at it.

The Caddy
You'll rarely find him and the clubs in the same place.

Sarah the Server
Who ordered the full roast dinner?

Brian the Barman
Who ordered the round of drinks?

The Souvenir Seller
He doesn't have a license to sell this stuff here.

The Angler
Loves to fish, but rarely has much luck catching them.

The IT worker
Always with a large coffee and hurrying to a meeting.

The Hiking Family
Mom and Dad enjoy long walks up hills and mountains. Their teenage children aren't so sure and they don't always stick with the group.

The Little Old Lady
She often has something unusual in her shopping cart.

The Little Old Man
Don't let that cane fool you - he's surprisingly nimble.

Fear Dearg
The wee red man who's always up to divilment.

Reilly the Robot
Sometimes it likes to dress up as a human.

The Shamrock,
The Headphones
The Lost Smartphone
The Magic Feather
These small items are hard to spot.

Green Level
Larry and family.

Bronze Level
These characters are easy to find.

Silver Level
A little trickier to locate this lot.

Gold Level
Tough - expert Larry hunters only!

COBH HARBOUR This is a fine hilly town, with lots going on! Cobh harbour is very busy with boats today – in fact, it's always been busy! Cobh is where lots of the nineteenth-century emigrant ships to America set out, as well as the ships full of convicts bound for Australia. It's also the last place the *Titanic* stopped before it went out to sea, crashed into an iceberg and sank! I'd rather keep me feet on dry land meself! For leprechauns, the best thing about Cobh is all the little streets and nooks and crannies – perfect for hiding me crock of gold!

RIENDS Gifts
CDS
OSING
ALE
TRINKETS
CORP
STOP
TAXI
OUT OF SERVICE

SKELLIG MICHAEL Watch where you're putting your feet when you climb up the steps on this rocky island – you could put your foot in a gannet's nest. Up at the top – 600 feet above the sea! – you'll find the little beehive huts built by the monks long, long ago – I remember them well, running up and down the steps in their brown robes. They weren't really men for the gold, they were more into their books. More recently, I was here, hiding in a hut, when some American film makers came – I hope they didn't leave any aliens behind them!

13

CLONMACNOISE This is a grand place, right beside the River Shannon where I like to fish. Many's the big salmon I pulled out of that river. Monks built the monastery here hundreds of years ago, and they must have liked stonework as there are so many carvings around the place that it would take you all day to see them! I like the two big round towers, meself, they're fine and private places for hiding whatever treasure you might have. I wonder who's hiding in them today?

WESTPORT HOUSE I remember it when the family of the great pirate queen, Granuaile, lived here – it suited them well, right beside the sea. Look out for the statue of Granuaile in the grounds; I always stayed far away when she was alive for fear she'd take me gold! Now there's a beautiful big house here and if you get tired looking at all the fancy rooms, you can go out and have a pedal around the lake in the famous swan boats or have a rest in the gardens. It's much more peaceful these days, and safer for a little leprechaun!

BEN BULBEN See the big mountain that looks a bit like a table? That's Ben Bulben – I'd say it could be haunted by the ghost of that poet fella W.B. Yeats. He loved it here. Well I remember him walking up and down reciting bits of poetry while I was searching for gold. I also bumped into Fionn Mac Cumhaill and his Fianna here long, long ago. They had their big hunting dogs with them so I had to hide till they'd passed by.

NO
TRESPASSING
7
21

DONEGAL CASTLE This used to be the finest castle in Ireland, but there's no royalty living in it now – they all left in the Flight of the Earls hundreds of years ago. They didn't actually fly away – they sailed out of Donegal Lough and found fame and fortune around the world. They saw a few places, let me tell you! I prefer to stay in Ireland, meself. There's enough adventure for me here!

SWAG
INCORPORATED

DERRY CITY WALLS Oh, I love Derry, so I do – there are fine big walls running all around the outside of the old city. Imagine that! You can walk along the top of them, looking down at all the action below, but be careful on the narrower bits unless you're as sure-footed as a leprechaun. Watch out for the cannons too, especially the big one called 'Roaring Meg'! And keep your eyes peeled for secret passageways!

MAGAZINE STREET
MUSEUM
Shipquay Place

BELFAST TITANIC Oh, it's very busy here these days with the Titanic Museum and the Wee Tram and all the tourists walking about. But it's always been busy, in the old days it was all hustle and bustle building ships – this is where they built the *Titanic,* the biggest ship the world had ever seen. But it hit an iceberg and sank not long after it set sail. Brr, that's why I keep me feet on dry land!

H & W
BELFAST tour
H & W
TITANIC

THE NATIONAL MUSEUM Janey Mac, it's a leprechaun's dream with all the gold here – I can't decide what to look at first, there are glass cases full of bracelets and earrings, necklaces and coins. There's even a little boat made of solid gold! It's enough to make me head spin! Just take care you don't get lost; you wouldn't like to be locked in here with the bog bodies!

DUBLIN CASTLE GARDEN

Did you know the name 'Dublin' comes from the Irish words 'Dubh Linn' or 'Black Pool'? This garden is where that black pool used to be. I used to fish in it! Now it's a park in the middle of Dublin, a fine, private place to while away some time counting me gold. But watch out for the snakes on the paths!

KILKENNY CASTLE Kilkenny's a great hurling county, but any hurler would have to be careful not to break all the windows here at the castle. The Castle has a ghost – The Blue Lady – say 'hello' if you see her. My favourite part is the forest in the gardens. There are loads of hidey-holes in the trees – as long as a nosey squirrel doesn't steal what I've hidden there.

23

HOOK LIGHTHOUSE Look out for the giant whales in the sea around Hook Head. And the seals and divers. And I'm always expecting to see another Viking longship; the water's very busy here and always has been! I stay well away from it – the big waves could wash a little leprechaun away! The black and white striped lighthouse is a fine place to visit, with its big, bright light to warn ships away from the rocks.

DANGER
STEEP CLIFF

Larry's Relatives

Each location also contains one of these relatives of Larry's. Read their biographies below to give you some clues as to which scene the character is hidden in.

Laurent
He escaped during the Flight of the Earls and went on to become a winemaker in France.

Larrus Leprechaunus
This relative annoyed the monastic scribes so much they drew him into the lettering on a holy book. He's very fond of his initials.

Lariella
She knows all the secret passages in and out of a city surrounded by walls. If you listen closely you can hear the tap of her hammer ... or is it her high heels?

Lars
This relative heard the Vikings were robbing all the gold so he stowed away on a Viking longship to Norway.

Larriam
A sensitive soul still believed to be working on his 10,000-verse epic nature poem. Wild countryside is his greatest inspiration.

Larook of the North
She was rescued from a very large sinking ship by some Eskimos and stayed with them in Arctic Canada – until she got tired of whale blubber.

Lur
A caveman leprechaun who lived in Ireland when it was all trees and stones. He was very happy when the first gold was discovered and made into ornaments.

Larrig
This odd relative of Larry's has many trained gannets on his island and it's said he wears a feathered coat to enable him to fly.

Laretta
She loves to sail the open seas and plunder the cargo of other boats – particularly when that cargo is gold.

Larrikin
A convict leprechaun who was forced to emigrate to Australia on a prison ship. Once there he escaped into the outback and hasn't been seen since.

Lally
This relative loves swimming and has a special suit made of fish scales. Back in the day Lally used to swim in the original 'Black Pool'.

Lar-Jay
The first leprechaun to hurl for his famous hurling county. He's not the biggest hurler ever, but he's fast.

Checklists

Even **more** things for Larry-watchers to look out for!

Cobh Harbour

- ❑ a musical sailor
- ❑ a sea horse and jockey
- ❑ a dog climber
- ❑ a cat fish
- ❑ patching a boat
- ❑ a painting of Larry
- ❑ a painting of 'Help!'
- ❑ a seashell boat
- ❑ a baseball player, a hurler and a hockey player
- ❑ an octopus in a net
- ❑ a big cake

Skellig Michael

- ❑ people in a cave
- ❑ a litterer
- ❑ the queen bee
- ❑ a stone carver's mistake
- ❑ seagulls taking a lift
- ❑ a climbing knight
- ❑ a spare head
- ❑ a broken unicycle
- ❑ flowerhead man
- ❑ a remote-control plane and a remote-control tank
- ❑ a message in a bottle
- ❑ a dragon
- ❑ a missed target
- ❑ six monks

Clonmacnoise

- ❑ a water skier
- ❑ a face in the tree
- ❑ a banana skin
- ❑ a fish-eye lens
- ❑ a sunbather on the roof
- ❑ a dog in a backpack
- ❑ a missing shoe
- ❑ two triangular hats
- ❑ a TV in a ruin
- ❑ a vampire on a roof
- ❑ five skateboarders

Westport House

- ❑ big and small lawnmowers
- ❑ a big dog in a small car
- ❑ a giraffe in a coach
- ❑ an elephant in a window
- ❑ a number of sausages
- ❑ a cool dog and a hot dog
- ❑ a big Q
- ❑ a washing line on a boat
- ❑ two large phones
- ❑ a big bar of chocolate
- ❑ four swan boats
- ❑ a cat boat
- ❑ a troll under a bridge

Ben Bulben

- ❑ a sheep with a backpack
- ❑ a black sheep
- ❑ ten rabbits
- ❑ a wolf in sheep's clothing
- ❑ a sheep in wolf's clothing
- ❑ a tank
- ❑ a hedgetrimmer haircut
- ❑ an owl
- ❑ five squirrels
- ❑ a tractor getting a tow
- ❑ a wild boar
- ❑ a bull on the loose
- ❑ a sheep with a quiff
- ❑ three bears

Donegal Castle

- ❑ a bouncy castle
- ❑ a tree castle
- ❑ knight vs caveman
- ❑ three heads stuck in a fence
- ❑ a unicorn
- ❑ a bird king
- ❑ a dog with an icecream cone
- ❑ a lizard with an icepop
- ❑ a large snail
- ❑ a large map
- ❑ a toy train
- ❑ a high diver
- ❑ a lute player

Derry City Walls

- ❑ a log roller
- ❑ candy floss hair
- ❑ a round car and a square car
- ❑ a man in a barrel
- ❑ a large dice
- ❑ two men in boxes
- ❑ two large eggs
- ❑ a worm in an apple
- ❑ a butter churner
- ❑ a pig in a window
- ❑ a bird with shopping bags
- ❑ a fiddler on the roof
- ❑ a bird watcher

Belfast Titanic

- ❑ a tug of war
- ❑ bed pushers
- ❑ a tandem bicycle
- ❑ a ship in a bottle
- ❑ the mer-family
- ❑ Samson and Goliath
- ❑ ice hockey players
- ❑ a fold-up bicycle and a fold-up car
- ❑ a cat with a backpack
- ❑ a car on legs
- ❑ a remote-control drone
- ❑ a monster truck
- ❑ a big bag of chips

The National Museum

- ❑ the bog zombie
- ❑ a large pint
- ❑ a fish tank
- ❑ a robot on tracks
- ❑ a penny farthing
- ❑ a giraffe
- ❑ a snoozer under a ramp
- ❑ a sleeping dragon
- ❑ a smiley mask
- ❑ a dog stealing a hat
- ❑ a gold key

Dublin Castle Garden

- ❑ a basketballer
- ❑ a big snake tail and a big snake head
- ❑ ducks in a paddling pool
- ❑ two men in two bins
- ❑ a plane and a canoe on a roof
- ❑ a deckchair
- ❑ burger vs sandwich
- ❑ a soccer game, a rugby game and a baseball game
- ❑ three vines and three tentacles

Kilkenny Castle

- ❑ the Blue Lady
- ❑ squirrels in a car
- ❑ a sheep in a window
- ❑ a blue man
- ❑ a Kilkenny cat, a Kilkenny dog and a Kilkenny mouse
- ❑ a window repairman
- ❑ a wooden castle
- ❑ a polo player
- ❑ a submarine

Hook Lighthouse

- ❑ a large torch
- ❑ a small whale
- ❑ a seal on an envelope
- ❑ a space ship
- ❑ a dragon and a sea serpent
- ❑ a rock band
- ❑ an ice-cream boat
- ❑ a fish car
- ❑ a monk's bonfire
- ❑ a long ladder

Expert Larry Hunters

Did you find **all** four single gold coins in each scene? One scene has **six** gold coins – but which one?

Many characters not on the lists appear in more than one scene. Only **one** unlisted character appears in **every** scene. **Can you find them?**

(***Hint:*** *the character has two tails and mischevious feet ...*)

First published 2016
by The O'Brien Press Ltd.,
12 Terenure Road East,
Dublin 6,
D06 HD27,
Ireland.
Tel: +353 1 4923333;
Fax: +353 1 4922777
E-mail: books@obrien.ie
Website: www.obrien.ie

ISBN: 978-1-84717-745-2

Colouring by Ken Mahon
Artwork Assistance by Declan Carroll

10 9 8 7 6 5 4 3 2 1
20 19 18 17 16

Printed and bound in Poland by Białostockie Zakłady Graficzne S.A.
The paper used in this book is produced using pulp from managed forests.

Published in:
DUBLIN
UNESCO
City of Literature